THE DAY THE LIFTING BRIDGE STUCK

THE DAY

BRADBURY PRESS • NEW YORK

Maxwell Macmillan Canada   Toronto
Maxwell Macmillan International
New York   Oxford   Singapore   Sydney

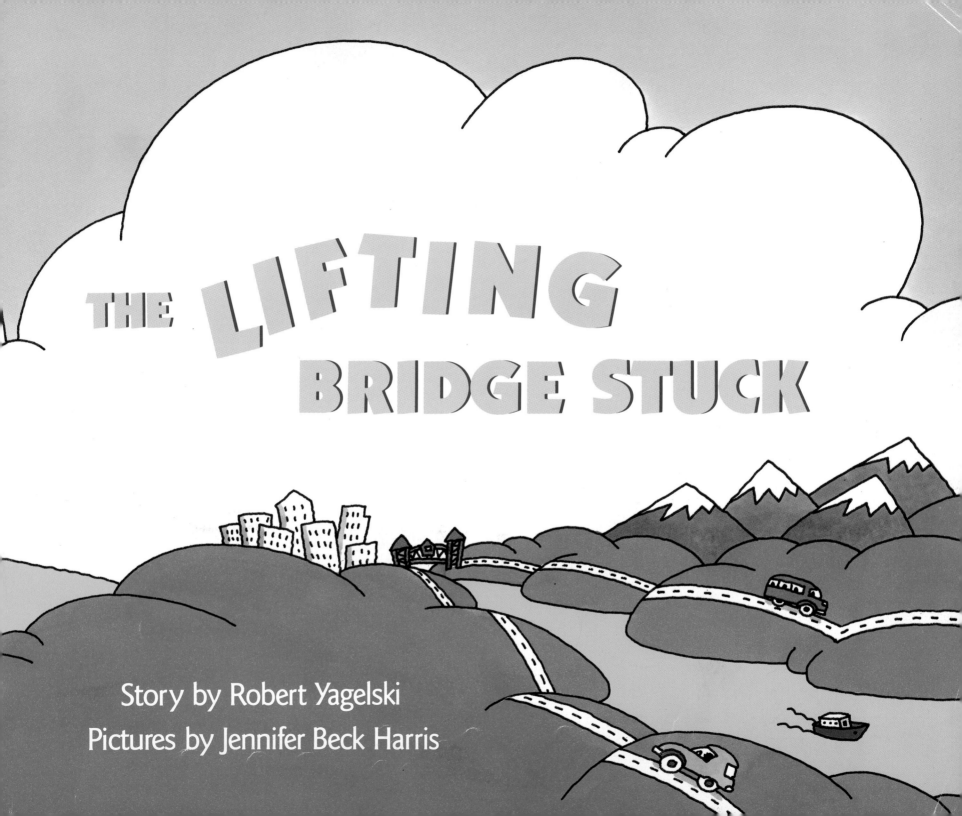

THE LIFTING BRIDGE STUCK

Story by Robert Yagelski
Pictures by Jennifer Beck Harris

Bradbury Press
Macmillan Publishing Company
866 Third Avenue
New York, NY 10022

Maxwell Macmillan Canada, Inc.
1200 Eglinton Avenue East, Suite 200
Don Mills, Ontario M3C 3N1

Macmillan Publishing Company is part of the Maxwell
Communication Group of Companies.
First American edition
Printed and bound in Hong Kong by
South China Printing Company (1988) Ltd.
10 9 8 7 6 5 4 3 2 1
The text of this book is set in Goudy Sans Book.
Book design by Julie Quan

Library of Congress Cataloging-in-Publication Data
Yagelski, Robert.
The day the lifting bridge stuck / by Robert Yagelski ; pictures
by Jennifer Beck Harris.
p.   cm.
Summary: Old Joe's lifting bridge is kept very busy as vehicles
drive over it and boats sail under it, until the day the bridge gets stuck.
ISBN 0-02-793595-7
[1. Bridges—Fiction.] I. Harris, Jennifer Beck   ill.
II. Title
PZ7.Y129Day   1991
[E]—dc20   90-33984

A NOTE ON THE ART
The illustrations in this book were drawn with black pen on Arches hot press
watercolor paper and then colored using Dr. Martin's dyes. The finished illustrations
were color-separated and reproduced using four-color process.

To Adam and Aaron, my best buddies,
whose love of stories
has inspired mine

—R.Y.

For Gramma, with love

—J.B.H.

Every day, cars and trucks drove over the lifting bridge to get from one side of the river to the other. Every day, boats motored under the lifting bridge to get in and out of the harbor.

Old Joe was in charge of the lifting bridge. He made the bridge go up and down. He made sure that everybody got to where they were going.

In the morning when Captain Pete chugged up to the lifting bridge in his tugboat, Old Joe pressed the switch that rang the warning bell. Red lights flashed.

All the cars and trucks stopped. Next, Old Joe pulled a lever to make the bridge lift high into the air. When the bridge was high enough, Captain Pete chugged under it and out to the harbor. He was on his way to help bring the big oil tanker into the port to unload its oil.

Captain Pete tooted his whistle as he chugged by.

Toot, *toot!*

Then Old Joe lowered the bridge. Now the cars and trucks could drive over the bridge again.

Betty Brown, who loved to sing, drove her bus full
of kids over the bridge on their way to school.

Rocky drove his tank truck over the bridge on his way
to the docks to pick up a load of oil for the service station.

Fisherman Frank drove his old Chevy over the bridge
on his way to the docks to get his boat ready for fishing.

chirp

Farmer Jake drove his pickup truck over the bridge
to the service station to fill up two barrels of oil
for his farm machines.

Mary zoomed her blue sports car over the bridge to Farmer Jake's farm, where she ran the farm machines that harvested the vegetables.

Chet drove his tractor trailer over the bridge to the grocery store to deliver vegetables from Farmer Jake's farm.

Doctor Paul drove his little red-speckled hatchback to the animal hospital to check his patients.

And on Tuesdays, Mrs. Mabel drove her green station wagon over the bridge on her way home from the grocery store where she bought vegetables.

honk

toot
toot!

The day the lifting bridge stuck, everything stopped.
The warning bell clanged and the red lights flashed,
but the bridge stopped halfway between up and down.
No matter which switch Joe threw, or which lever he
pulled, the bridge wouldn't budge.
Nobody could get to where they were going.

Captain Pete couldn't chug his tugboat under the bridge.

squirt

Farmer Jake and Chet couldn't drive their trucks over the bridge. Betty Brown couldn't drive her bus full of kids over the bridge. She stopped singing. Dr. Paul couldn't drive his red-speckled hatchback to the animal hospital.

w h i z z z z

w o o f

groan

Rocky and Fisherman Frank and Mary were all stuck, too.

Mrs. Mabel honked her horn.

Even Andy, who came from over the mountains and who had never seen a lifting bridge before, couldn't drive his big rig over the bridge to deliver his apples to the grocery store.

Everybody was stuck.

squeak

Old Joe turned his wrench.
Nothing happened.
Old Joe turned his wrench again.
Everybody waited.

tweak

Slowly the bridge began to move.
It lifted higher in the air.
Everybody cheered.

Captain Pete chugged his tugboat under the bridge to bring the big oil tanker into port to unload its oil.

Then Old Joe lowered the bridge.

Rocky drove his tank truck to the docks to pick up oil for the service station.

Betty Brown, singing again, drove her bus full of kids over the bridge to school.

Farmer Jake drove his pickup truck to the service station to get oil for his farm machines.

Fisherman Frank drove his old Chevy over the bridge on his way to his fishing boat.

Mary zoomed in her blue sports car to the farm to run the farm machines that harvested the vegetables.

Chet drove his tractor trailer to the grocery store to deliver vegetables from the farm.

Dr. Paul finally arrived at the animal hospital.

And Mrs. Mabel made it home with her groceries just in time for a picnic.

Old Joe smiled.
Everybody got to where they were going...

even Andy, who delivered his apples to the grocery store and then drove his big rig back over the mountains, where he told everyone about the day the lifting bridge stuck.